STORY BY
DAVE EGGERS

ART BY
KELLY MURPHY

L B

LITTLE, BROWN AND COMPANY

NEW YORK • BOSTON

LUCIAN LIVED WITH HIS MOTHER on a windswept shore. After storms, he roamed the beach searching for faraway things. That's what his father had called whatever washed up from across the sea: faraway things.

One morning, after a swirling storm full of lightning and thunder, Lucian walked the beach, hunting for something new. He found a trio of jellyfish, looking like tiny blue moons. He found a heavy red rope tied tight in a knot.

Then he saw something bright.

It was wrapped in seaweed that was dotted with hollow pods, but he freed it and held it high. It was silver and gold and copper and was finely etched all around. It was a kind of sword he'd seen in books, but he couldn't think of its name. He swung it left and right and tried to remember the word.

Not *saber*. Those were longer. Not *foil*. Those were skinny, almost weightless. It wasn't a machete or broadsword or claymore.

Then he remembered. *Cutlass*. He slashed at the sky and the word seemed to emerge from the vents he'd made in the clouds.

"Cutlass!" he yelled.

"What's that, son?" his mother yelled from high above.

"Nothing," he said.

He climbed the bluff and brought the cutlass inside
and asked his mother if he could keep it.

"Is it a faraway thing?" she asked.

"Yup," he said.

"It's not owned by a neighbor?" she asked. "Or left by a visitor to the beach?"

"It's a faraway thing," he said.

He'd never seen anything like it.

In his father's old
toolbox, he found the right
hardware and two long nails, and
he hung the cutlass on the wall in his room,
across from his bed. He stared at it for an hour before
sleep overtook him, and when he dreamed, he dreamed
of his father. He often dreamed of his father, and these
dreams stayed with him, and became memories, and these
dream-memories became, in Lucian's mind, almost as
real as his real memories, which he worried were fading.

The next day, Lucian spent his time in the tide pools, on the bluff and in the coves, always with his cutlass in his hand or fastened to his side.

He used the blade to cut driftwood and seaweed,

and once he even cut the sun
in two like an orange.

(It recovered.)

All day Lucian slashed and felt strong and purposeful. Only one time did he miscalculate and turn one of his sleeves from long to short.

That afternoon, as the fog over the ocean cleared, Lucian saw a great wooden ship. He expected it to move across the horizon, but this one was still, as if its eyes were fixed on Lucian.

A rowboat was lowered from its side to the sea, and Lucian thought it impossible that the crew aboard would be visiting his remote and rocky shore. But the boat came closer and closer.

A splotchy dog leaped into the shallow surf and ran to Lucian, circling him like a tornado. Three figures followed and walked with long strides up the beach. Lucian stood absolutely still. He tried not to be afraid because he had his cutlass with him and, just minutes before, he'd cut the sun in two.

"What happened to the lighthouse?" asked a man with very large glasses and very large arms and a voice of authority. Lucian took this man to be the captain and knew he should answer, but he couldn't find the words.

"Sure could have used that lighthouse two nights ago," the captain mused. "Got caught on a sandbar, and we've been digging our way off it ever since. I even lost my—"

And then the captain's eyes fixed on the cutlass in Lucian's hand. Lucian moved the sword behind him protectively, and the captain sighed. "I don't know how to say this, but that cutlass you're holding is mine."

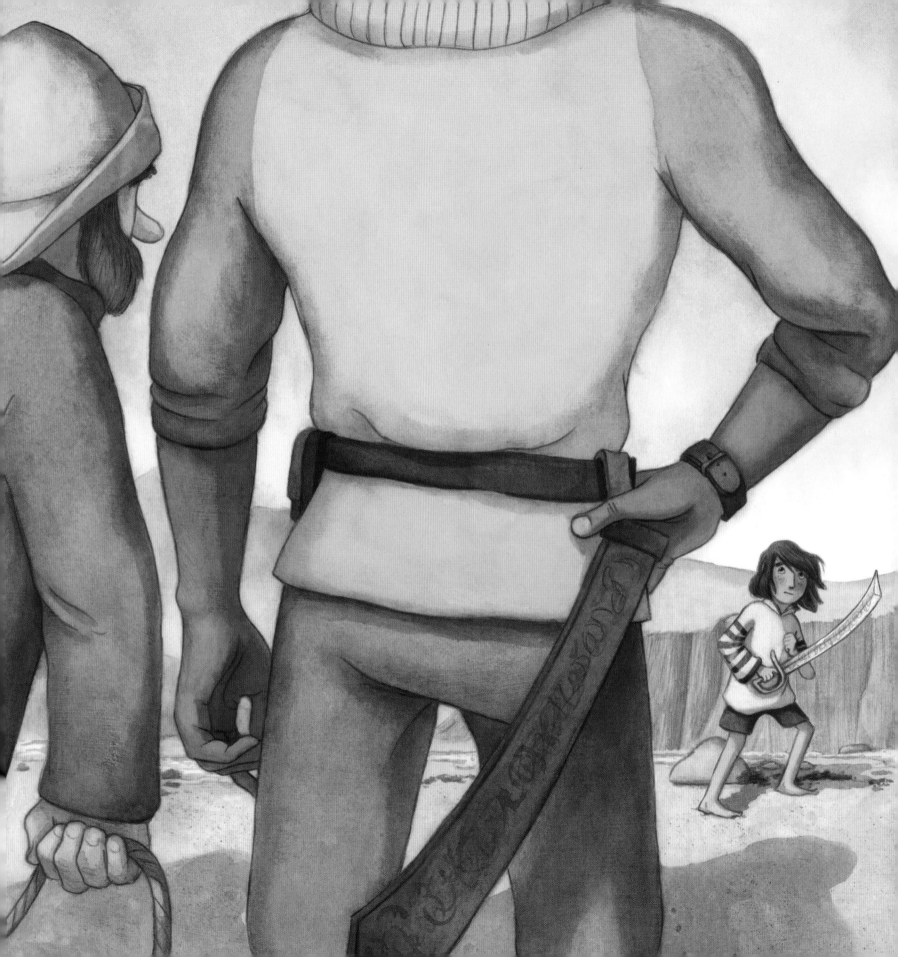

"Sorry," Lucian said. "This is mine." But while he spoke, he saw a sheath hanging from the captain's belt. The sheath had designs carved into its leather that mirrored the ones etched onto the cutlass blade.

"Listen," the captain said, "I want to offer you a trade. If you return the cutlass, I'll let you choose whatever object you like from the treasures I've accumulated. That cutlass means more to me than anything on my ship."

Lucian looked back at his house above the bluff. His mother wouldn't approve, but he knew what he had to do. He tied his own rowboat to the captain's, and he followed the captain, his crew, and the splotchy dog out to the ship.

As they got closer, Lucian saw a few dozen crew members working to free the ship from the sandbar. They were prying and hammering and pushing, and took little notice as the captain helped Lucian up the rope ladder and onto the galleon.

The captain led Lucian to the stateroom and opened the delicately decorated double doors. Inside, Lucian saw a feast of glittering objects. There were hexagonal coins and a silver sextant, a collapsing telescope and a falconer's glove.

Lucian studied the treasures for something to replace the cutlass. A dagger? A saber or broadsword?

"Choose wisely," the captain said.

But one object spoke to Lucian more than any other, and when he chose it, the captain smiled broadly and lowered it from the high shelf on which it sat and put it into Lucian's small hands.

"Thank you," Lucian said.

Lucian gave the cutlass back to the captain. "Thank you," the captain said, and slid the cutlass into its sheath.

From outside the stateroom, there was a loud cheer from the crew. They had freed the ship from the sandbar.

Lucian climbed the rope ladder down to his skiff and waved to the captain and crew, and they waved back. And even before Lucian was ashore, the captain and his crew had opened their sails to catch the wind and were gone.

"Is that you?" his mother asked when she heard the screen door clap shut.

"It is I," Lucian said, though he'd never said that phrase before. It sounded both right and funny, and when his mother laughed, Lucian laughed, too.

"What do you have there?" she asked, looking at the lantern in his hands. "Another faraway thing?"

"Sort of," he said.

Lucian told her the story of the captain and his crew, and the ship and the sandbar, and the captain's complaints about the lighthouse with no light.

"Can I go up to the tower?" he asked, and she said he could.

So Lucian ran up the spiral steps of his father's lighthouse, and at the top, he lit the lantern and placed it by the window, where it turned the ocean silver and gold and copper and even, for a moment, touched the last of the captain's ship as it disappeared beyond the never-ending bend of the sea.

ABOUT THIS BOOK

The illustrations for this book were created with acrylic ink, gel medium, pencil, and watercolor on paper. This book was edited by Andrea Spooner and designed by David Caplan and Kelly Brennan. The production was supervised by Patricia Alvarado, and the production editor was Jen Graham. The text was set in Baskerville, and the display type is Baskerville.

This book was aided by the input of the Young Editors Project, a program that invites young readers to see manuscripts-in-progress. The author would like to thank these young editors: In Austin, Texas, from the Austin Bat Cave: Isabella, James, Samuel, Aaliyah, Mia, Lilyan, Elon, Bianna, Daniel, Genesis, Delilah, Lucia, Michelle, and Anisha. And from the fourth-grade class at Mountain View Elementary School in Lacey, Washington: Alyssa, Maurice, Zoey, Vara, Logan, Kymani, Luke, Adriel, John, Craig, Devin, Valor, Iris, Cameron, Deja, Adrien, Joshua, Chloe, Lucas, Vida, Cameron, Ava, and Kaeden.